*

GO BEYOND

By

J.J. BHATT

ISBN:

9798853238169

Title:

Go Beyond

Author:

J.J. Bhatt

Published and Distributed by Amazon and
Kindle worldwide.

This book is manufactured in the Unites States of America.

Recent Books by J.J. Bhatt

HUMAN ENDEAVOR: Essence & Mission/ A Call for Global Awakening, (2011)

ROLLING SPIRITS: *Being Becoming* /A Trilogy, (2012)

ODYSSEY OF THE DAMNED: *A Revolving Destiny,* (2013).

PARISHRAM: Journey of the Human Spirits, (2014).

TRIUMPH OF THE BOLD: *A Poetic Reality*, (2015).

THEATER OF WISDOM, *(2016).*

MAGNIFICENT QUEST: *Life, Death & Eternity,* (2016).

ESSENCE OF INDIA: A Comprehensive Perspective, (2016).

ESSENCE OF CHINA: *Challenges & Possibilities*, (2016).

BEING & MORAL PERSUASION: *A Bolt of Inspiration*, (2017).

REFELCTIONS, RECOLLECTIONS & EXPRESSIONS, (2018).

ONE, TWO, THREE... ETERNITY: *A Poetic Odyssey, (*2018).

INDIA: Journey of Enlightenment, (2019a).

SPINNING MIND, SPINNING TIME: *C'est la vie*, (2019b).Book 1.

MEDITATION ON HOLY TRINITY, *(2019c), Book 2.*

ENLIGHTENMENT: *Fiat lux*, (2019d), Book 3.

BEING IN THE CONTEXTUAL ORBIT: *Rhythm, Melody & Meaning, (*2019e).

QUINTESSENCE: *Thought & Action,* (2019f).
THE WILL TO ASCENT: *Power of Boldness & Genius,* (2019g).

RIDE ON A SPINNING WHEEL: *Existence Introspected, (*2020a).

A FLASH OF LIGHT: Splendors, Perplexities & Riddles, (2020b).

ON A ZIG ZAG TRAIL: *The Flow of Life*, (2020c).

UNBOUNDED: An Inner Sense of Destiny (2020d).

REVERBERATIONS: The *Cosmic Pulse,* (2020e).

LIGHT & DARK: *Dialogue and Meaning,* (2021a).

ROLLING REALITY: Being in flux, (2021b).

FORMAL SPLENDOR: *The Inner Rigor,* (2021c).

TEMPORAL TO ETERNAL: *Unknown Expedition,* (2021d).

TRAILBLAZERS: *Spears of Courage*, (2021e).

TRIALS & ERRORS: A Path to Human Understanding, (2021f).

MEASURE OF HUMAN EXPERIENCE: *Brief Notes,* (2021g).

LIFE: An Ellipsis (2022a).

VALIDATION: The Inner Realm of Essence (2022b).

LET'S ROLL: *Brave Heart,* (2022c).

BEING BECOMING, (2022d).

INVINCIBLE, (2022e)/ THE CODE: *DESTINY,* (2022f).

LIFE DIMYSTIFIED, (2022g) / ESSENTIAL HUMANITY, (2022h).

MORAL ADVENTURE, (2022i / SPIRALING SPHERES (2022h).

EPHEMERAL SPLENDOR, (2023a) / CHAOTIC *HARMONY*, (2023b).

INTELLECTUAL MYSTICISM (2023C) / WILL TO BELIEVE (2023D)
EXPECTATIONS & REALITY, (2023E) / THREAD THAT BINDS (2023F)
ONCE & FOREVER, (2023G) / PERPLEXED, (2023H) / GO BEYOND.

PREFACE

Go Beyond boldly affirms that the awakened human existence is a logical necessity to champion the meaning, "Self-Truth." In that context, our collective journey of the "Global Spirit" must triumph over endless conflicts: subjective judgments, fickle opinions and the age old belief-based frictions; resulting into bloody violence's , wars and even genocides as lucidly demonstrated *via regia* historic experiences and even by the events that are happening in the contemporary times. It is therefore, paramount, we bring our collective common-sense together and seek, "How to reset our sanity in this otherwise obfuscated reality where human existential uncertainty remains sovereign!"

J.J. Bhatt

CONTENTS

Go
Beyond

Let I
Go beyond and
Be the cosmic
Spark forever

Let I
Explore
All the unknowns
Far from this noisy
Milieu

Let
There be right
Rhythm, melody and
Meaning while I journey
Through my time

Let I've
The moral courage
To reach my
Ultimate Truth, and be
Free from the noisy
Milieu…

Once
Alive

Shadows
Robbing his
Once cherished
Memories

He's running
Away from loving
Ones already;

Enfolding
Slowly within
The world of his
Big void

That is the
Stateless mind;
Not knowing,
"Who he is"

That
Was my old
Friend, once a highly
Honored man;

Helplessly,
Falling into the
Grips of a deadly
Mental nemesis...

Endless Battle

No matter,
How hard you try
To clear the cloudy
Affairs and still there
Is no resolution

Indeed,
How fast you try
To walk through the
Muddy waters, but the
Will doesn't want to
Go along

Intelligent
Beings though aware,
"What is the core issue?"
Fails to adapt for some
Odd reason

Intelligent
Beings striving to
Be confidence of their
Noble Mission, and still
Unable to fulfill the
Set goal, but why?

Pernicious

Sinners
They are,
For deceiving
Young girls; turning
Them into victims in the
Name of their insane
Belief

Killers
They are,
For murdering many
In the name of their
Out dated thinking

Deceptive and
Cruel they're for not
Obeying,
The Golden rule
Of humanity

Be aware
Of their violence
And the 'Double talks;'
Still peddling same game
Of the old revenge…

Forever

Is it not
Time to enjoy
Beauty and truth of
Our romance in
Waiting?

Is it not
Time to smile and
Dance to the endless
Journey of you and me

Come,
My lady, let's just
Forget all our troubles
And fly off the edge,
And be happy
Ever in the lapse of
Our never ending love

Yes dear Heart,
Let's be in love forever,
And be free from the
Long waited feelings,
At, once…

Adventure

Life,
What an adventure
Where simplicity
Keeps ascending to
Complexity, and

Unity seems
Disintegrating into
Diversity and chaos

That's where
Human struggles
Begins and keeps on
Time after time

Life,
Always a vulnerable
Blue print; undermining
Moral endeavors

Life,
What a consequential
End; either a mirage
Or a big riddle!

Significant

Significant
Being, always
An inspiring gift

He got the
Strength to vibrate
The mighty universe

He got the
Audacity to ask,
"What is it all about?"

Significant
Being always a
Magnifique Soul;

Rolling
Through the
Timelessness of
All there is

Significant
Being, it's high
Noon to rise and be
The savior of your
Own misdeeds…

New Trail

Humanity
Be a one mighty
Unity of
All possibilities

Let it
Reshape the world
Toward goodness;
Setting the stage for
Children to live well

Let it
Be the chief mission;
Redefining an effloresce
Destiny of humanity in
Return

In other words,
"Let's be motivated,
And begin the walk
And no talk…"

Moral
Call

Amid
Violent
Milieu our time,
Let, every
Caring soul take
A moral stand and

Fight
Back to ensure,
"Humanity is on the
Right track"

Freedom is
Safe when each
Takes his/her social
Responsibility at
Every turning point

In other words,
When inner erosion
Of the will occurs;
Social strength diminishes
In time... defeating the
Very purpose of,
"Civilization..."

Sometimes

Sometimes,
I think, am lost in
The world
That seems
Dying under its own
Inglorious blunders and
Sins

Sometimes,
Am concerned,
"If any basic civility
Been saved to honor our
Existence as intelligent
Beings"

Sometimes,
I think, "We're the
Blind "Time Travelers,"
Not knowing where we're
Heading?"

Sometimes,
I try to triumph over my
Anxiety and uncertainty of
Tomorrow, but it never shows
Up while am still awake…

Let Time Flow

Lovers
May think they're
In love forever, but
There can take a sudden
U-turn

In any case,
Lovers often remain
Uneasy and being
Complex even with
Saccharine chats and
All the big dreams

Being in
True love is not an
Easy experience;
Keeping feelings so
Fresh forever

Oh yes,
Lovers don't ever
Brag, they silently
Enjoy the feelings of
Trust and respect…

Revival

Who
Doesn't hold hope
Must be a greatest
Tragedy to exist

Let him
Have courage to
Revive, rejuvenate and
Resurrect his will to
Win the game

Human
Without a goal is
Another tragedy that
Got to be resolved
Through
Self-confidence;

Knowing,
"Who
Really he is, and
Where is his right
Track to roll?"

Voyage

Every time,
I flipped through the
Pages of history,
I reckon,
It's my voyage
Through the turbulent
Mighty Blue Sea

Every sentence,
I read and realized,
There is nothing but
Mostly blood stains
And false narratives;
Writing the script

Not a pleasant
Experience,
"Humanity's been
Repeatedly wounded
By the greedy few"

Time
To rewrite a new
Story, and let there
Be enlightened beings;
Leading the world toward
Simplicity and wisdom....

Necessary Logic

Our first
Axiom be coherence
And clarity of thought

That be the
First step along the
Trail to enlightenment

That be the
First call to "Becoming"

Let each human
Be the rhythm, melody
And meaning in the
World he/she's walking
Through

Let's never
Forget, "Human,
What a marvelous
Continuum civilization,
Time after time, indeed."

The
Magic

Love,
What a mystical
Magic; epitomizing
My core essence

Life,
Also another
Splendid chance to
Fall in love,
Unexpectedly

Laughter,
The power behind
My spirit; letting me
Keep rolling through
All imperfections

Love, life and
Laughter, what a
Wonderful way to
Be natural human
To be forever…

One
Mission

Time to
Recover from the
Historic wounds

Time to
Address the
Contemporary issues

Time to
Think of children's
Future today

Time to be
Separated from
The old habits of
Seven sin

Time to
Walk together
With a single mission.
"How to save the planet
And humanity, today."

Authentic

In that
Bucolic country,
Two innocent
Young hearts were
Strolling through the
Blessed zephyr from
The high hills

For them,
The turbulent
World was not there
As they kept enjoying
Freedom with no
Interferences

Well,
In that
Pastoral beauty of
Their first kiss,
They silently
Understood depth
Of the genuine love
With no disturbances,
At all…

The Passage

Young braves,
Keep the journey
Rolling

Keep the curiosity
Exploding and

Keep the confidence
Growing

Remember,
Life is always a
Thematically invoking
Discourses

To know the
Self well while walking
Along the challenging
Track as ever

Let your
"Inner lens," reckon the
Beauty of, "All That is."

Natural

Awakened
Human is the best
Miracle to be

Let him
Soar through the
Scurrilous skies and
Be ebullience of
His worthy time

Let him
Know, "Existence
Never a moral static, but
The best experience,
It always is"

Let him,
Keep exploring
All the pleasures of
Life, but sharing 'em
With others as well,

I mean,
Life after life;
Sustaining,
"Humanity to its best."

That's Life

Each is a
Consequence
Of choices that
Made earlier

Each is
Caught between
Between,
"Good and evil"

Each is an
Adventurer of the
Unknowns, always

Each
On the battlefield of
Life and death from
The very beginning

Each must
Keep rolling forward
With a strong will to be
The winner in the game,
As intended to be…

Return

Being
Immersed into
Silence of the night
For a very long

Please,
Do awaken
His slumbered
Spirit

I say,
Dawn's already
Broke and why is he
Still at sleep?

Why is
He not grasping,
"His future is
Running away from
His big dream"

Please,
"Wake him before
He turns irrelevant
In the game that's
Already been set."

Betrayal

Human
Must remain
Inseparable from
His moral spirit;
Sustaining logical
Box to keep moving

Duality
Was a nasty blunder;
Letting Mother Nature
Lose the child

As a
Consequence,
The child grew-up
Ignorant and quite
Arrogant to be

Leading to
Million assaults
Choking his own
Mother to near death!

Sadly,
He still remains obtuse;
Failing to take care of
The dear Mother…

Noble
Great

To be
Living as a
Human is a
Greatest gift of
All

For he
Alone got the
Power to justify,
"Moral Truth"

Human is
The prima facie of
His magnificent
Quest

Let him
Keep rolling.
Let him
Keep exploring.
Let him
Keep "Becoming."

Being & Essence

It's the
State of "Unmind"
That's the real climb

It's the
Full focus on the
"Truth" that maters
The most

That's how
Being is ready to
Conquer the meaning
Of his existence

Let him
Open-up new trails
Where others would
Walk through and

Be
The humans larger
Than ever before…

Turn
Around

Is there a
Way to freedom from
The cage full of myopia,
Phobia and revenge

How one should
Cleanse the corrupted
Mind, and learn how
To behave
In modern world

Given
The state of
Brains-washed
Thick heads, "How
Do we awaken their
Common sense"

The question,
"How do we reform
The unfit ideology and
Turn it around; bringing
New intelligent humans
To the modern world…"

Don't
Run

Don't you
Run away from
This man without
Confessing face to
Face,
"You don't love
Him anymore"

I say,
Don't ignore your
Real feelings and tell
Me, "You don't love
Anymore"

How can you
Separate two souls
They've been one
Forever!

How can you
Just walk away knowing,
"You're lying to your soul?"
Don't betray love
For we've been one throbbing
Heart from the very first kiss…

Best
Gift

Life
Though a greatest
Miracle of all, is a
Uncharted blueprint

It's the
Curiosity or at times
Anxiety keeps stirring-up
The silent thoughts

Life
What a magnificent
Walk from innocent to
Myriad experiences and
Still not knowing,

"What is the
Very meaning of all
That was, that is and
What shall be?

Life, what
A best gift to
Grow from ignorance
To an illumined mind,
Forever.

Let's
Roll

Let's join
A noble mission;
Letting children
Proudly declare,

"We're
Born to make
A positive difference in
This troubled world"

Let's walk
Through the dry
Terrain and dig deeper
To bring water at the
Surface; letting hope
Grow to the
Thirsty billion others

Let's light-up
The world with one
Mighty slogan,
"Humanity above all"
And let's be
Free from the insanity
Of the seven sin at last.

Toward Freedom

When
We're reduced
To simplicity
At that
Turning point,

We
Shall be walking
Along a right path
Where pure essence
Shall inspire us all

Time to
Free ourselves from
Hypocrisy, social ranking,
Constant deception and lies

Time to be
Enlightened and pass
Through the patches of fire
With calm and full-confidence
As a unifying collective strength...

Salute

Great minds:
The Vedic sages,
Plato, Shankar, Kant
And many others inspired
Me to think along perennial
Riddles of human quest
To know the self

Even the
Great quantum thinkers:
Schrodinger, Heisenberg,
Many others concluding;
A rational compatibility between
The Vedic conceptuality and
Scientific awareness, today

The Vedic
Thought understood,
"Consciousness is the Anthrocosmic
Link with the Eternal Consciousness,
"Brahman thus it never dies."

Today, science concludes,
"Consciousness is information
And it never dies but retained in
The Universe forever."

Enigma, or Dilemma

In this
Constantly revolving
"Thought world,"
Where issues of
Existence and

Its validity
Has been explored
For millennia and still
Certain answers remain
Mute

Why the
Difference between
Subjectivity and objectivity
When in the end, it's all
One absolute nothing!

I mean,
When all finite realities
Are dissolved into the
"Eternal Nothing," where
Do we seek our collective,
"Truth!"

Moral
Good

Human
Excessive greed
Hurt others

That's why
Responsibility and
Self-restraint is very
Essential

I mean,
In the name of
" Good of the
Whole as always"

Let us
Discipline our minds
And look above the
Self-centered gains, but
For the sun shine of a
Tomorrow's world…

Not Yet

When
AI's and OI's
Begin to rule the world

Wonder,
"How will children
Discover the meaning
Of their freedom?"

If the
Universe is unreal
As the noble laureates
Declared,

Wonder,
"How shall we
Justify our existence?"

If the
World is dying in
False beliefs and
Utter revenge,

"How shall we
Fulfill the universal
Spirit of love?"

Wake-up
And Go

It's
Incumbent upon
Us to understand the
Moral value of our
Modern time

Otherwise,
The pendulum shall
Swing back to the
Stone Age!

It's time
To awake and let the
Collective will win the
Battle on-hand from this
Point on

Time to
Master the new rules
Of the modern game and
Just move on to be genuine
Being again…

Spinning

In this
Blowing storm of
The modern time;
Have we forgotten the
Inner courage or what?

In this
Fast changing state
Of the world;
Have we lost our habit
Of adaptability or what?

In this
Techno-mania realm;
Are we facing, two
Human species,
"Organoid high IQs
And the rest other us,
Humans or what?"

Isn't it time
To understand and
Save our collective
Moral significant at this
Turning point or not!

Be the Heroes

Let there
Be sanity and
Clarity of collective,
"Good"

That got to be
One way to keep
Reverberating the deaf
World

Let's know,
"There can't be fulfillment
Of the ultimate wish without
Morality, reason and justice
As our priorities"

Time to
Roll-up the sleeves;
Bringing harmony, hope…
Integrity of the mind

Time to
Drop the old diabolic
Habits of yesterday, and
Time to walk forward with
The heads-up today…

In Their Names

All we should
Care is how to leave a
Gift of moral inspiration
To the young

Our historic
Hands been bloodied;
Let it not pass onto them

I mean,
Let them grow-up with
Greater vision of a
Peaceful world

No it's
Not a utopian craze,
Albeit a bold adventure
For young to move from
Sheer ignorance to be smart
Illumined human beings…

Recollection

Oh yes,
At times,
I do think of that
Beautiful far land
Where I was born

From where
Millennia ago,
Some of the greatest
Humans emerged on
The scene; directing
World to walk along
A moral track

Yes,
They're my Vedic
Ancestors and am proud
Of their gift of wisdom
To the world

Oh yes,
They're my inspiration as
I recall memories of my
Far beautiful land…

Soaring
Giant

Oh that
Far land now a
Rising star after
Long struggles

Salute
To such fearless
Over billion souls

Still
Fighting against
Evil forces of the
Time

Yet
Moving forward
With self-confidence
And good intention

Indeed,
The God sent Hero is
Fostering a noble
Spirit: *One world.*
One family. One future.

Clarity in Order

Not waiting
To glimpse eternity,
But a determined will
To thrive in it

Not waiting
For truth to be explored,
But to be experienced
All of it

Not waiting,
"What you think
Is pertinent, but
What you do good
To others is"

Not waiting,
To worry of AI's and
All other such gimmicks,
But to seek ways to control
Them to save our collective
Freedom is…"

Uphill
Climb

Walking
Through the
Trial & Error trail,
Nothing seems
So certain anymore

What's the
Point preaching the
Dated messages
From the old books

What's the
Point adhering to the
Failed habit of deaths
And destructions

I say,
"What's the
Point; preaching
False narratives

When human
Still got to climb
The steeped hills,
To be Good again!"

Straight Talk

I've
A sneaking suspicion,
Of these AI's and so on
Being imposed
Upon us under the
Disguise of so-called,
"Progress"

Seems, it's all about
How to control the
Mind of the masses

Yes
To undermine our
Freedom, our identity,
Our dignity and thus our
Very humanity indeed

What if
These few modern
Techno oligarchs are
Brining alive,
"The Orwellian Ghost or
What!"

Dear Lady

Dear Lady,
What a wonderful
Walking beauty you're

Please,
Don't rot into that
Cruelty, vanity or
Greed again

I say,
"Don't smear your
Sacred soul and
Alienated from the
World again"

Come,
My dear lady and
Be the wonderful
Walking beauty you've
Been always

Please
Wake-up and
Be the loving heart
You're before…

Remember

How do
I take off the
Edge and be the
Moral will

While I
Ascend to the
Realm of many
Unknowns

How long
Do I keep ascending?
While I carry this pulse
Of history in-making

I never think,
To quit the scene
Even I've to keep
Flying higher than
Where I've been

Yes, I've
Greater responsibility
Over freedom so
I can win over my
Set goals in the realm
Of many unknowns…

As
Always

Dear Heart,
Today we're taking
This sacred vow to be
One forever

And that's the
Way our solemn
Journey must begin
As of today

Let this
Moment seize our
Grand story to sing;
The lyrics of trust and
Friendship

Dear Heart,
So long we're the
Union of our moral
Strength and the power
Of our will to be ever

We shall win
All the challenges on
The way and transcend to
Eternity as one…

Power
To be

Those are
Real heroes
Who can break out of
Their fear and despair
With full awareness

Let the world
Be reverberated,
"Human identity
Must be grasped
With respect to
His true humanity"

Time
To inspire children,
"How to be calm and
Self-confident and

Move-on with
Full-confidence against
Million odds and still be
The victors until the end…"

In
Love

And now
Is the time to bid
Goodbye for a
While to all the
Sweet memories

That's the
Way, the story of
"Love and death"
Seems all about

That's the
Lyrics of our long
Lasted romance;
Coming to an end

Don't tear,
Don't despair for
Love never dies

Dear Heart,
I shall be
Waiting in eternity
To honor our earthly
Vows.

Lift off

How do we
Drop
This hedonistic
Lifestyle and
Soar to the
New heights

Let's
Immersed in
Strengthening our
Moral will to be
The victor at last

How do
We rise above this
Cacophony and the
Seven sin and

Be the
Winner in lifting
Humanity to its
Ultimate magnificence!

Never Ends

Mortal beings
Looking for
Immortal Truth

Mortal beings
Not knowing the
Trail is too long

Mortal beings
Walking along a
Highway of many
Unknowns

Meanwhile,
Chaos and dark
Remain sovereign
In their thick heads

All seems
So bleak and there
Is no light to guide, but to
Interpret   the subjectivity
Of all that is, indeed.

Greetings!

Why
Build a world
Where greed undermines
The power of humanity

And, what is the
Point in living within
The great sphere of,
"False narratives"

What's the
Reason, "Why be in
A reality, where most
Feels forlorn from their
Humanity?"

I mean.
"How do we defeat
The enemy whose
In each of us?"

What if
We recapture,
Our lost simplicity, and
Be free from our hellish
Mentality?

We shall

Time to
Take a new trail
Where we've chance
To grow-up being wiser
Than wounded historic
Experience

Yes,
Time to know well,
"Where to go?" and
How to move on and
Be happy again

Let it
Be the awakening of
Our "Global Spirit"

Let it
Be the quintessence
Of our collective
Journey through these
Trying times, indeed...

Ascension

Keep
Flying higher and
Higher 'til there is
Neither triviality nor any
Negativity to disturb the
Silent soul

Keep
Walking miles and
Miles 'til there is
Neither violence nor any
Senseless war to disturb the
Very "Goodness" of every
Peaceful being

Keep
Exploring million
Different paths, and
Discover one that
Takes humanity to the
Realm where our
Ignorant minds shall be
Illuminated at once…

Born to
Win

Let us
Grasp, "All that is"
Must be in the thought
Only

Indeed,
Being is the epicenter
Of thought-provoking
Earthquakes; discovering
Bit by bit,
"What is and what is
Not with each jolt"

In the final
Analysis,
"Human is the measure
Of his morality, reason
And vision of all that is"

Let him be
Aware. Let him grow and
Let him glow all the way to
His deep meaning…

Discovers

Understanding is
The first light that
Let you
Destroy evil within,
In an instant

It's a
Moral courage
To know the Self is
First reason to be
Worthy to exist

Indeed,
It's the purpose well
Served, if hope is shared
With billion others during
The barreling killer storm

Let us all
Touch the beauty of
Truth and know the
Value of existence in
This potentially good
World...

Resurgence

Amid darkness,
Folks may soliloquy,
"Why
Just live moment to
Moment when
Nothing to be gained
While the ride is on"

That is the very
Defeatist attitude and
Doesn't do good to
Any one, but them

Humans
Not just keep walking
Toward despair forever

They must
Own a moral will and
Rational insight to be
Bold ever

Yes, dare know,
"How to play the game
And be the winners at last…"

Complex
Web

My finite
Consciousness is the
Real connectivity
With the infinite
Riddle already

Yet
The clarity is
Missing from the
Anthrocosmic link

In such
A state of ambiguity,
How do I restore;
Mind to its original
Source?

That is
The fate of "I," who is
A consequential being;
Struggling with pure grief
And still seeking his
Cosmic aspiration, indeed…

Illumination

Come,
Let's be proud
Of whom we're

We're
Endless sparks of
The brilliant light

We're the
Eternal essence
Being human

We're the
Outward projections
Of, "One Soul"

We're
The images of
Perfection, we've been
In search for sometime...

Ethical Judgment

At the
End of the day,
"Our meaning turns clear
From knowing the self,
Well"

As we bring
Hope and happiness
From our thoughts,
We're embolden with
All our possibilities

While
Passing through the
Dark patches, important
To keep the disciplined
Mind steady

Do remember,
We're the live conceptuality
That observes, understands
And builds a vision,
"What's right and what's not…"

Lost
Time

Between
The journey from
A small town to the
Mighty and complex
Big cities,

Many million
Dreams have flown
Through, and

Never resting
To think in full
Tranquility,
"What is it all about?"

While
Chasing the brilliant
Stars and ambitions;
Time slipped way so
Soon, and

Never got the
Chance to say in-person,
"Goodbye to mom and
Pop and some siblings…"

Endless

Every passing
Second, I am evolving
From nothing toward
Something

That seems
To be my continued
Experience either through
Every night or every day

Perhaps,
That's the perennial
Cosmic experience,
I've been ordained
To go through

What a
Giant but complex
Ever growing spider
Web,

Seems,
I've been trapped
Since beginning of
Every new beginning…

Dear
Heart

Don't push
Me over the edge
Don't throw
Me into despair

For am
In love with you,
Dear heart

Yes, I wait
For your
Every pulse is
My heart throb

Yes,
Dear Love,
You're the light
Giving meaning to
Live

I say,
"Come back and
Let's go back where
We left the trail
We're on before…"

Two
Buddies

Being
Ever so tightly
Bounded by two
Buddies:
Life & Death

Life
Never offers a
Guarantee, but
Gives all the thrills
To be alive

Of course,
In life struggle means
Understanding value of
The precious time

Life, what a
Sealed matrix
Where grief and joy
Keeps dancing

While
Death opens a
Way to the million
Unknowns, beyond.

At the Fork

When
Cause and
Consequence turns
Zero, nada or zilt
We enter the
"Eternal Tranquility"

Where
"Nothingness" is a
Weird reality yet it's
A deep meditation

In such a
Inscrutable experience,
Wonder if the Super
Being is happy or not?

What
If the familiar
Existence with all the
Disturbances, pleasures
And pains

Be more exciting
Than that spinning
Sphere of the prodigious
Unknown Bliss!

Equipollent

From
Very conception,
The blueprint seems
Already in action

Pre-registration
At a prestigious
Kinder garden and
Then at a prestigious
Big school and so on

Even
The child is imposed
With so many rules and
Regulations from parents,
Teachers and coaches

Sometimes
All goes well when
Child turns teen, but
At times all such
Wishes may backfire

Oops,
The young rebels;
Shattering big dreams
Like a house of cards…

One
World

We're
Journeymen walking
From imperfection toward
Perfection either knowingly
Or unknowingly all right

We've
Evolved from being
Insignificant to be significant
Through our historic struggles,
Blunders and a few inglorious
Sins as well

Time,
We're concerned with our
Contemporary responsibility
And begin a world of, sanity,
Unity and dignity to save
Our identity, our humanity,
Indeed

Time,
We lift children's dreams.
It's time
We lift the world above from
It's misdeeds and be inspired again…

Point
Upward

Whatever
Born shall die and
May or may not return

However
Ignorant being may be
Time to be evolved
And illumined

Whoever,
Slices, dices and
Grasps got the
Chance to open
The door to the self

In other words,
Time to learn the
Meaning, "What is it
All about?'

Time to
Shred off all the
Old habits of violence,
War-mongering and
Get back to the right
Track again…

Seize the Moment

Why
Let go existence
For nothing
When reality is so
Generously;

Offering all
The beauty, adventures
And endless curiosities
To be fulfilled

Why don't
We sing and dance
With inspiring lyrics of
Love, laughter's and life
And seize the moment,
Now

Why don't
We keep soaring
To the unknown realm;
Gaining some wisdom
As our best experience!

Fly High

Perhaps,
On other side
Of the unknown,
Where life and death
Remains neither

I mean,
Where life is dead,
And dead means
Being alive

Where
Everyone is a
Single spark of
Moral Will

In such a
World of different
Dimensions,

We're all
Our paradoxical
Miracles as we try to
Catch truth out there
Far beyond, when it's
Already within…

It's Happening

Watch out,
We're being
Swept away by these
Powerful waves of
Mighty struggles and
False narratives

Watch out,
We're succumbing to
The inevitable forces of
Change; eroding our
Freedom so silently

Yes, our
Future is in danger
Indeed as children may
End up living in an alien
World of AIs and with it,
All bets may be off...

Mélange

There is
Light and there is
Dark

There is
Life and there is
Death

There is
Good and there is
Evil

There is
Human and there is
Blind belief too

There is
Reality and there is
A quest to know it all

There is
Humanity and there is
Negligence to its dignity,
Too!

Socratic Irony

Be bold to
Ask right questions;
Unfolding contradictions,
Paradoxes and riddles
From the opponent

Demand,
Explanations to
Set the stage to show
Limitations and scope
Of the pretenders

Do carry-on
Conversations; revealing
Fallacies of those who
Consider to be so pious

Go quiz the
Intelligentsia and
Measure,
"What they're
Saying either right
Or otherwise."

That's
The Way

Learn to
Take love, life and
Narratives with a
Pinch of salt

Nothing is
Perfect and guaranteed,
Only disciplined thoughts
And deeds shall free the
Solemn soul

Learn to
Enjoy whatever
Time is left and be in
Full gratitude always

You're an
Ordinary being who is
A base-reference
From whom, all successes
Is measured time after
Time…

Second Thought

Looking
Through mental
Lenses,
Reality seems
Chameleon day after
Day and

Paradoxically,
Nothing changes at
Prodigious depth

While
Exploring the realm
Of myriad unknowns,
Curiosity remains
Sovereign, yet
Little is revealed in
Return

How many
Tomorrows to wait
Before we're victors
In the great game of
"Ignorance & Arrogance."

Reality: Not 20/20

It's
Illusion of real love
That betrays two
Sweet hearts, in this
Age of hedonism

Even
The blind trust in
A given belief turns out
To be most destructive
To the whole

Profiteers,
Bend backward
In making profits
For them alone and not
For the social well being

That's the
World we've been in
That's how
Humans shall continue
To be

Unless young shall be
Morally guided from
The very beginning…

Off
The Edge

Why
Existence be
Obsessed with
Judgmental calls

As if
There is
No other way to
Seek harmony and
Happiness

Why be
Critical of life
That's been unfair
Since the start

As if
We, half-animals
Have been powered
By the perfect mind

Why fall
Into such a trap
When human
Identity hasn't met its
Full- expectations yet…

Love
Essence

Dear Soul,
We've been
Journeying all along
Since the first sparked
Feelings called, "Love"

Remember,
Love is either
A heavenly experience,
Or a cruelty of insecurity
With million tears to drop!

Dear Soul,
Our rides been both;
Making us better lovers
Than ever

Thanks to your
Understanding and
Patience
Thanks to your
Deep courage and
Timely wisdom,
We're still
Journeying through the
Power of love, love...loves.

Illumined

Being
Caught now and
Then by the
Merciless spinning
Cycles of uncertainty

He's seeking
Escape from the
Gathering killer storm

Being
Trapped deep into the
Dark cave; asking to
Exit as soon he must

Let him enjoy
The beauty of sunny
World … the magic of
Endless creative thoughts

Let him be
The image into
Eternity where he can be
His own perfection at last…

Moral Courage

When fearless
David stared at giant Goliath face to
Face and uttered, "I can take him"
That was his moral courage in action

When
Fearless Satyagrahis (Peace
Protesters) fighting for India's
Freedom faced armed Brits, the world
Understood what a moral courage is
In action

When Civil Rights
Protesters faced the wild
Dogs and bursting hatred, they
Remained calm; showing their
Moral courage in action, once again

When in
Tiananmen Square, that one
Unknown protester; standing before
An on-coming tank to crush him,
Remained calm and unperturbed;
Demonstrating the world his
Moral courage in action…

Be What
You're

Just
Buckle-up and
Keep flying higher
Than ever before and

Enjoy the
Lovely ride all the
Way to your deserving
Freedom

Be what
You're and don't
Imitate, but help lift
The world with your
Ingenuity and boldness

I say,
Enjoy the magnificent
Quest and be
An eternal being through
Your own good
Deeds…

Think,
Now

As state of
Imperfection keeps
Spinning into the
Mind of every sentient

Wonder,
"Isn't it time for them
To go beyond the edge?"

Hey good
Friends and foes alike,
"Isn't it time to live for a
Greater goal ever than
Before?"

In this
World of fear and
Anxiety, ""Isn't it time
To hold hands and be
Walking for best times
To our children
And theirs to come!"

Anthrocosmic Link

As I stare
At the magnificent
Cosmos where zillion
Unknowns keep smiling

In such a grand
State, am being bathed
By a constant
Stream of inspiration;
Stirring-up my
Dormant will at once

I feel
All the eternal
Forces strengthening
The moral will;
Awakening my core
Essence on the spot

Yes, that is
My miracle to be human;
Who's connected with infinite
Possibilities of his own...

Closure

At this turning
Point of my life;
Getting ready to
Close the book, but
Before let me recollect
A few memories:

I stand
Alone before the
Holy waters of the
Land I was born

Remembering, my
Arya ancestors from
Whom I carry their
Blood line

While my
Eyes are shut and
Silently facing the first
Rays of the rising Sun,

I dive into the
Holy world; closing
The Great Cycle of my
Seventy-generations in
An instant and now am
Ready to leave the world…

Rolling
Storm

We're
A giant moving
Storm through chaos
And beauty at the
Same time

We're
A giant confused
Box locked-up with
False narratives peddled
By the defunct beliefs

We're
Searching our
Lost simplicity, family
Ties and real freedom from
The techno- mania all right

Oh yes,
We're born natural moral
Beings, but who're failing
To conquer our collective,
"Integrity of the mind…"

Conscience

Echoes
Knocking the thick
Heads of the mortals,
Everywhere

Yes,
Echoes from
Historic experience
From the
Contemporary scene
From the
Failed common-sense

Echoes
From the cosmos
Echoes
From the unknowns
Echoes
From the inner being,

Asking to wake-up,
Arise and get on with
The mission of all that is
Beauty and truth...

Core
Essence

If we're
Born to be humans,
We should never lose
Our moral destiny

For that would
Be the only way, we
Shall save our kind
And the planet itself

Let us
Be empowered by
Our infinite possibilities
And the indomitable will;

Making it all
Through today, so a
Good tomorrow belongs
To the young forever.

Miss Awesome!

Hey you,
Awesome
Beauty named,
"I Don't Care"

What a
Lovely is your
Sweet smile
What a
Thrill is to see you
Every day by the
Main gate

Your
Perfect physique
Glowing with all that
Confidence and arrogant
Flare is so impressive
Indeed

I wait everyday
By the gate just to
Say, "Hello," but you
Never cared, "Either am
Dead or alive?"

Keep
Moving

Go on
Without fear or
Anxiety ever

Just keep
The focus steady
Against cacophony
Of trivialities and
Toxic people

Ignore
"Nay sayers" and
Keep the journey
Going without any
Interruption at all

That's the
Secret to your
Ultimate
Success in life

That's the
Way to gain confidence
And be a trail blazer; leaving
It opens to the billion others…

Silent
Force

Every human
Is a live struggle
And even despair while
Being in an imperfect
World

That's the
Royal road to resolve
The formidable puzzle
What is a desperate search
For truth

Nothing is
Worth when not
Earned through
Blood, sweat and tears

Time to
Relearn, how to exists
With a positive stride,
And be proactive with the
Rules of the unfair game

And all throughout,
Be a silent force to take
The world along a right trail...

Thread
That Ties

Love, yes love
That's what shall
Heal the suffering
World today

Love is the only
Thread ties all our
Differences and we
Become caring humans

Love,
What a common
Destiny from all
Senseless conflicts

Love,
That's the real truth;
Making us better mortal
Beings

Love,
I mean the
," Selfless love"
What a best essence
Ready to be shining for
Many tomorrows to come…

Apathy

Are we
Still waiting to ignore,
How mankind is conceding
To the smart machines?

Why there is no
Open protest against
It, I mean to save our
Freedom?

Where is
Our fearless spirit,
To save our identity,
Our dignity and our very
Humanity, "Who we're
And what we can become"

What are we
Doing by being so docile
While our collective dreams
Are silently fading away day
By day to the emerging
Non-human thinking machines…

Mental
Gymnasts

Intelligent
Being caught
By the state of either
Illusion or reality

I mean,
He's churning into
The mega-machine
Of nova trends;
Forgetting his
Original identity and
Purpose of existence

Oh yes,
He's trapped between
Illusion and reality, and
Not reckoning,

"It's
All a mental
Gymnastics being
On the highway of
Myriad unknowns only…"

Progress or Regress

If the world
Keeps moving from
Mankind to the thinking
Non-human machines

Wonder,
"What is the meaning of
God, immortality, piety
And so on?"

What if,
The future is evolving
Over a fragile thread;
Breeding more machines
In number than our kind

I mean,
"What would be the
Real meaning to exist in
Such a non-human world!"

Deadly Game

Every now and
Then we suffer for
Our repeated blunders
And sins

That's been
The general saga since
The beginning and the
Bleeding continues even
Today

Whenever
Wealth and power
Falls into the hands of
A few

That's when
The consequences of
The set game begins
Without any blame or
Guilt to report!

Change
The Script

Let's
Roll forward,
"Where every child
Is groomed to be a
Noble being indeed"

Let's
Build a world,
"Where moral will is
A norm and not an
Exception to the rule"

Let's
Be bold and begin;
Erasing carcinogenic
Violence's, bigotry and
Wars in our time

Why should
We let go our dream,
Our awakening and

This very
Common magnificent
Destiny; embodying
Our collective truth?

Cave Dwellers

Though we're
A juggernaut
Historic force

Do we
Ever care to know,
"We're the agents of
Change?"

Do we
Ever care to pick-up
The torch, and
March for a better
Future for our kids

Do we
Ever learn to
"Point Upward"
Instead, blaming

Each
Other of our
Built-in collective
Imperfection!

Responsibility

When
All is in flux and
All ebbs and flows,
Where
Do we seek a steady
Place; regaining our
Lost moral being?

When
This journey is
All about change from
Ignorance to awakening,

How do we
Regain our rational
Goodwill
To build better us!

No, it's not
The easy way to the
Divine, but got to be
Responsibility of each
While struggling to walk
Along a right track…

Reflection

We're humans
Who're caught by
The forces of history
And modern trends

It means,
Existence not as rosy,
But a swinging pendulum
Between, "Beauty and
Thorn, indeed"

Perhaps,
We're in this
Realm either being
Intentional or accidental,
And that enigma yet to be
Unlocked

Oh yes,
We're humans born
To wake up and must learn
To walk along a track; leading to
Our collective enlightenment...

Declaration

Let the
Young blood boil-up
And reverberate the
Deaf world:

We'll fight to death.
We'll not let AIs govern
Our freewill's

Come,
What it may, we'll not
Run away from our noble
Call to save freedom

Of course,
We'll not surrender our
Spirit to build a better
World

Damn right,
We'll fight to the last
Drop to reach our final
Goal, "Not to be the slaves
Of the these growing nemesis,
"The mega-thinking-machines..."

Love
Endures

As we
Keep soaring higher
And higher in the
Beauty of our love and
Trust

Sweet Heart,
We've become the
Wheels of immortality;
Spinning life after life

What a
Fascinating experience
It is; loves shining with
Every big dream through
Timelessness of all that is

Yes,
Sweet Heart,
Our story is the eternal
Beauty of trust and
Pure friendship
So I sing,
"Keep the wheels of
Love spinning forever…"

Destiny

Human
Alone is the player
In this on-going
Universal epic

For he's the
Generator of ideas,
Opinions and crazy
Whims; seeking truth

He's
The quintessential
Emotional intensity, who
Keeps stumbling over
Good or bad as ever

Human,
What a
Formidable payer
In the universal epic;
Fighting to know,
"What life is all about?"

Beware

In this
Chameleon world of
Constant,
"Ups & Downs,"
Existence be a firm
Self-affirmation

Let us
Consecrate our
Lives to a noble cause
To know the depth of
Our moral possibilities

Existence,
If driven solely by
Greed and narcissism,
Inevitably shall kill
All our big dreams

Let existence,
Be self-purpose and
Substance to direct us
Toward greater good
Of the whole always…

Identity

I am,
What I've become
While walking through
This flat or rough terrain
Of my experiences

I am,
Who's not afraid
To take on the imperfect
World and be the winner
With full-confidence

Though I am,
A momentary flash
Between birth and
Death only

I am,
What life gave it
To me time after time

In the final
Analysis, I am
The expression of
My identity, my dignity…
My humanity…my
Own moral being…

My
Journey

I contemplate
To reinvigorate my
Moral being only

I sing to build
Better thoughts
Within

I write
To express feelings
And deep concerns to be
Shared with all others;

Opening-up
A few dialogues to know,
'Where're we heading?"

Oh yes,
Life got a purpose.
It's all about illumined
Minds to destroy ignorance
And fire-up young braves to
Be enlightened forever…

New Path

If
Darkness keeps
Looming over our
Thick-heads for a very
Long time, means
We must be collectively
Rolling toward a wrong
Direction

If
We read
Our history full
Of blunders and sins,
Means we've great deal
Of work do in our time

Time to
Open-up a new chapter
Time to
Change the attitude and
Be active today

Yes, time to
Rewrite a new book
Titled, "How to coexists
As Responsible Moral Beings…"

Task
Ahead

In the end,
We must be the
Redeemers to fix
The damage done

To our
Precious humanity
Through long passage
Of the past

And the past
Chasing the present,
And in turn impacting
Future of our children

Let
Us stand up and
Hold a fearless state of
A Global Spirit and

Begin the
Process of healing to
Regain
Our forgotten identity
As intelligent beings…

Miss Beautiful

Hey my
Dream gal,
When will you
Come down to the
Reality of waiting
Love

Hey
Stubborn gal,
When will you give
Your sweet smile again

Every day,
We meet at the college
And even in every class,
But you don't care to look
At me once

Hey
There beautiful gal,
When will you say,
"Hello with a sweet smile,
At least once!"

Nameless

Why keep
Rotting in this
World of violence's,
Disorder and wars

Why
Insult our
Common goodness
And keep suffering
Forever

Let's
Get off the
Cage and let's get
To the work

Let's drop
All belief spawned
Confusions, lies and
Deceptions, and conclude:

"There is
Only ONE known
By different names…"

Out of
Hell

Disunity is
Killing our dreams
Disunity is
The enemy One

Disunity is
The first cause of
Our suffering,

It's bred
From ignorance,
Indifference and greed

Come,
Let's use our common
Sense to save the future of
Our kids

Come,
Let's walk in the name of
Our moral call to build,

"A milieu of
Stability, peace and
Harmony to the whole."

Nova
Path

Children
Don't fall in the
Same trap as your
Elders

Children,
Read and understand
History well, I mean
To get the truth from
In-between the lines

Children,
Begin to grasp the
Root causes of the
Turbulent world and
Learn,
'How to eliminate 'em
On reaching adulthood"

Children,
No apology shall ever
Come from the guilty elders.
Just drop that expectation, and
Keep on opening up new trails…

Great
Sphere

Time to
Seek clarity and
Time to focus on
The inner being

Time
To drop old dated
Judgments and redefine
The journey ahead with
A larger perspective

Time to greet
Others as good friends
Instead, being strangers
To them

That would be
The beginning of our
Rational dialogues, and
Moral intensity to live in
The world of goodwill for a
Change...

The Direction

Love,
What a miracle
Of two throbbing
Hearts

Who can't
Wait to dance out
Their sweet dreams

Love,
What a magic
Between two waiting
Souls

Who can't
Wait to begin their
Journey of big dreams

Love,
What an eternal
Reality of two blended
Solemn souls…

Being &
Meaning

What if,
Eternity that feeds
Time

What if,
Being is the real
Spark

Who's born
To know genuine
"Self"

What if,
Human is the
Pure paradoxical
Riddle itself, and

Who's
Born to clarify
All that stated while
The rough ride is on…

Apotheosis

Let
Life be lived with
A magnificent rhythm,
Melody and meaning

Let it be
The song of every
Heart, mind and
Goodwill Spirit

Let each
Be a metaphysical
Reality, albeit a living
Poetry, and

Conquer the
Integrity of the mind
Yes, to be triumphant
As an enlightened being

Let each
Be fearless and genuine
And dare," Go Beyond
Illusion and deify his/her
Soul…"

Heroes
On the Go

Go catch
The distant brilliant
Stars and

Ride them
To explore farthest edge
Of the bubble, and dare
To know the truth

Go catch
The golden Sun and
Shine every child's
Hope to live well

Don't be
Afraid, buckle-up
And save the Planet Blue
And every life there on

Go catch
The bull by the horn
Called, "The seven sin,"
And save all that is,
"Moral Essence of every
Human soul…"

Perspicacious

It's always
A great thought that
Leaves a permanent
Memories to enrich
Our existence bit better

While
Standing before
A great art; stirring
Up deep feelings of
Our admiration

While
Listening to a
Mesmerizing music,
We dive into an instant
Deep meditation and

On reading
A quality book;
Giving a keen insight

That's how
It's best to grasp,
"The Self and the
Complex world around,
Bit by bit…"

Love,
Demystified

It's
The unexpected,
Call it," A spontaneity
Of romance"

What may be an
"Epiphany of love"
That never leaves the
Stirred-up heart

Love,
What a magic force
Binding two lovers
Forever

Love,
What a fire that
Can burn two lovers
Either way forever

Love,
What a capricious
Gift to hold onto ever…

Noble Mission

When an
Idea and reality
Fits perfectly well,

There emerges,
A logical closure and
That must be, I suppose,
"Truth"

When an
Idea is backed by
Moral intention and a
Supremacy of reason,

There must
Be an illumination of
The mind

With such
A simple understanding,
Let's get ready with a
Right blueprint and

Get to work
To finish the mission; we've
Been thinking for a long.

Toward Light

Uncertainty,
Subjective notions and
Fallibility of judgments
Remain so visible today

Wonder,
What happened to our
Commitment, "Be the
Social warriors of moral
Good?"

Why
Face this unnecessary
Uncomforted state of
The mind called,
"Suffering"

Let every
Sunny day turns into
Illumined thoughts,
Words and deeds,

And let's
Move on with such a said
Mission, every challenging day…

Big
Mirror

Hey folks
Did you know?
"Our sheer ignorance
Is killing the good name
Of Almighty, and our moral
Significance as well?"

Don't you
Think, "It's a serious
Issue to be resolved soon
Before we lose our humanity,
Or, what?"

Look at
Our collective images
Into the mirror called,
"Reality"

Do you
See, "How nonhumans,
We appear in it through
Our past and the present?"

Reliable
Pal

Ever since our
Two hearts began
To beat so instantly,
Loves been our
Reliable pal

Its love and
Nothing but loves
Only way to win
Our truth

So, I ask,
"Why are you waiting
Over there, and afraid
To take the first bold step?"

Dear Heart,
Love is a
Beautiful gift and

So is
This life meant for
You and me at this very
Moment of our youth…

Be
Smart

As existence
Flows forward,
Why hold thick layers
Of worries, tears and
Despair

Remember,
The rule 101,
"Life is but a
Love, laughter and
Hope"
Why then be
Alienated from the
Good world

It's our
Last chance to be
Humans while
Rolling from birth to
Death

I mean,
"Everything beyond
Seems only
A pure assumption!

Age of Info

Let's
Demystify all the
Grand talks, big ideas
And rigid preaching's

For they've
Delivered not much,
But confusion, division
And disaster

Just read
The world history
And you'll know,
"What's happening,
Today"

Be sure
To read the objective
Contents and gather info
From diverse sources

And arrive
At a logical conclusion
On your own, and not
That of any paid peddlers
Of a hidden propaganda

The Storm

What if,
Humanity is a
Mighty dust storm

Where
Irrationality, despair
And struggle keeps
Spinning at all time

Who knows, if
We're being blown
Away far from our
Moral being

Life what a
Dry terrain where
Not enough rain,
And we utterly remain
Where we've been

Wonder,
If anyone cares,
"If we're dying here
Or over there by the
Barreling killer dust storm…"

Culprits

Is there
Any reciprocity
Of "Goodness"
Left among folks
Of a dying Planet

Each silently;
Pushing so hard to
Dominate its narrative
While throwing dirt
At others

All guilty
Parties hiding behind
The scene; triggering
Hatred, violence and
Even wars

Time to
Ignore them. Its
Time to make them
Irrelevant and the world
Must move toward higher
Enlightened goals…

How Long?

Dear Lady,
Awakened is my
Soul through your
Miracle feelings
Called, "Love"

Awakened
Is our joint destiny;
Silently singing to
Celebrate our new
Romance

Time to
Wake-up from the
Deep dream
Time to
Be in alive in the
Magic called,
"Love"

Dear lady,
"How long will you
Keep dreaming while
I wait in the grips of
Uncertainty?"

One *vs* Billions

In this
Holistic Universe
Where the past, present
And even the unknown
Future seems bounded
Together by one fragile,
"Self-truth"

From such a
State of reality,
"There be equality in
Everything. There be
Goodness in
Every experience"

But then
Why there is
"No harmony,
Hope and positivity;
Inspiring
Billion young to
Point Upward!"

All Is
Unity

Contextuality
Is the mother of
All social dynamics
That is
Why most folks
Stick around in
Saving their sanity

Existence
Is cruel all right,
But it's a light and
Dark path wrapped
By many unknowns

Connectivity
With the self and the
Mighty universe is
The name of the game
Where holistic reality
Still to be fully known...

Fulfillment

There is
Courage and uncertainty
Hiding beneath every
Lover's heart

There is
A constant fear and
Anxiety while fighting on
That bloody battlefield

There is
A need to clarity
About love
While lovers keep
Walking along a trail of
False narratives

There is
A bold venture of
Love called, "Trust"
Let it be the focus
Of every participating
Lovers on the battlefield...

Nova
Inspiration

Come
Young braves,
It's time to go beyond
And probe the reality
Of many unknowns

Let it be your
Bold move
To throw away
All negative forces,

And to
Begin a journey of
New vision and of course
New attitude

Be fearless
To keep ascending
Toward the realm where,
"There is effloresce bliss and
Goodwill, always"

Take Note

Today,
Many millions are
Dying over-bearing
Emotional stress

Is it
A consequence of
Cheap junk food,
Insecurity or
Illicit drugs or what?

Take note,
Today many millions
Are "Climate refugees"
And they're desperately
Looking for help

Take note,
Today many millions
Using "Asylum; "abusing
The trust of host nations

Take note,
Politicians remain passive
To resolve those issues;
Protecting their voting-banks…

Turning
Point

Once
Innocent years
Fades away,
Every person turns
Into another

I mean,
Fed by love and
Hate; good and
Otherwise and so on

If one
Awakens in time
Well, he/she is an
Illumined mind and
The journey of meaning
Begins at that turning
Point

If not,
There opens a realm
Of alienation; defining
Complete failure of the
Human essence…

Introspection

Conception
Of the Divine is good,
If it strengthens
A genuine, "Global Spirit
For peace, stability and
Harmony of humanity"

Religion is
Okay so long it doesn't
Peddle false piety and
Promote forced conversion
Through deception or fraud

World conferences
And so-called, "Global
Forum" is useful, only
If each participant talks
Less and walks more

Let the arm-chaired
Intellectuals,
Go out in villages and
Help in elevating poverty,
Unhygienic, diseases and
Build schools and hospitals...

Issues

How do
We know our truth
And let the souls be
Free forever

How do
We govern our
Old habits of the
Seven sin and

Still
Gather necessary
Steadiness to win
The set goal

How do we
Submerged into the
Grand metaphysical
Poetry and

Be in the
Lapse of eternity to
Unfold meaning of
The Self and the
Great riddle,
"What is it all about?"

Being &
Journey

Volition,
What a wonderful
Gift to exercise our
Choices
While the ride is
On

Albeit,
That is the ultimate
Meaning of our own
Being in action

Oh
The freedom,
What a
Greatest validation,
"Who am I and
What I ought to be"

Vindication

Nothing else
More
Pertinent than
To be active with
A set noble goal

That gives
Direction to life,
Albeit a right
Step

To be in
Harmony with
All others including
The Self itself

Nothing else
Is more pertinent
Than be an awakened
Soul; lifting the
Inner spirits of
All that is, indeed…

Being &
Insanity

If the
World continuous
To implode
With its zillion tons
Of bad decisions:

Who knows,
Where shall we be
Tomorrow?

And to this
Recurring
Destructive habits
Of misguided humans;

How do we
Convince them,
"Humanity is eroding
And the Planet is
Slowly dying?"

Think
Smart

Just get
Busy to eradicate
Falsity and the
Myopic attitude

Let us
Regain to live,
"Best of who we're
Born to be"

It's a
Logical necessity,
And of course, a
Common sense,

"Why
Life be wasted when
We're the owners of all
That is, Good"

Let us get
Smart and redefine
Our common destiny
Before it's too late…

Human, Again

Time
To end this long
Charade of contrived,
Complicated conflicts
Of wars and greed

Time
To seek deeper
Meaning, "Who we're
And what we can become?"

Let us
Be brave to kill all the
Negative forces of our
Existence

Let us
Relearn how to
Breathe fresh air again.

Let us
Relearn how to drop these
Electronic gadgets for a
Change, and be humans again…

God, Demystified

God is a
Solemn journey of
All intelligent life
Grasping;

"What
We ought to be;
Honoring human
Dignity at all time."

God means,
Conquering the
Integrity of the mind

To comprehend,
"Why we exists and for
What logical purpose?"

God is our
Silent inspiration;
Enjoying harmony, hope
And happiness, life after
Life in essence."

Footprints

Everything
Seems
Independent and
Interdependent at the
Same time

We're
Independent,
Sensu strictu,
Only when we dream
Or make decision with
Certain set consequences

Otherwise,
We're constantly
Tethered
To the contextual
Existence all through

Until
Falling into the
Lapse of the waiting,
"Death."

Take Charge

What if
Our history lucidly
Depicts,

"The games
Been in action, but the
Rules been neglected
Time after time"

What if,
This world just a one
Big mad house; looking
For a good psychiatrist to
Cure its stubborn disease?"

Wonder,
"How long we keep
Dwelling into such a
Crazy place?"

Wonder,
"How long shall we
Ignore, well-being of
Our innocent children's
Future that's hanging
With myriad uncertainties?"

We're Real

Contrary
To the popular
Blind belief,

Life is an
Amazing, *tour de force,*
Let it be the path to the
Global awakening

Like to
See the world
Where each is measured
By the prodigious depth of
Hope and a great sense of
Social responsibility

Let us,
Keeps the gusto going
Let us,
Be confident to believe
In our meaningful destiny,
Forever ...

Global Force

When do
We begin our
Pilgrimage not to
Any divine place, but
To the sacred Soul

Yes,
That's the real
Source we must
Enter over and again

Let meditation
Through creativity,
Imagination or a moral
Inspiration lay open
The path by every inch

Come.
Let us be fired-up
To be larger than life,
Always

Let us be
Worthy of our births
Before hitting the exit Gate…

Being
In Love

Only
In your love,
There is beauty and
Truth; walking me along
The highway of
Endless fulfillments

It's in
Your magic smile,
I've been dancing into
Heavenly feelings as
Ever

Yes,
Dear Heart, "You've
Been my reality to be
Alive and happy forever..."

Please,
Don't run away from
The dream, I mean don't
Ever vanish from the
Reality we've been together
For many, many eons...

JAGDISH J. BHATT, PhD

Brings 45 years of academic experience including a post-doctorate research scientist at Stanford University, CA. His total career publications: scientific, educational and literary is 100 including 60 books.